WELCOME TO THE ANCIENT FAR NORTH . . . AND THE WORLD OF THE MICEKINGS!

WHERE THEY LIVE: Miceking Island

CAPITAL: Mouseborg, home of the Stiltonord family

OTHER VILLAGES: Oofadale, village of the Oofa Oofa, and Feargard, village of the vilekings

CLIMATE: Cold, cold, cold, especially when the icy north wind blows!

TYPICAL FOOD: Gloog, a superstinky but fabumouse stew. The secret recipe is closely guarded by the wife of the miceking chief.

NATIONAL DRINK: Finnbrew, made of equal parts codfish juice and herring juice, with a splash of squid ink

MEANS OF TRANSPORTATION: The drekar, a light but very fast ship

GREATEST HONOR: The miceking helmet. It is only earned when a mouse performs an act of courage or wins a Miceking Challenge.

UNIT OF MEASUREMENT: A mouseking tail (full tail, half tail, third tail, quarter tail)

ENEMIES: The terrible dragons who live in Beastgard

MEET THE STILTONORD FAMILY ...

GERONIMO
Advisor to the miceking chief

THEA
A horse trainer who works well with all kinds of animals

TRAP
The most famouse inventor in Mouseborg

BENJAMIN
Geronimo's nephew

BUGSILDA
Benjamin's best friend

. . . AND THE EVIL DRAGONS!

GOBBLER THE PUTRID
The fierce king of the dragons is a Devourer!

The dragons are divided into 5 clans, all of which are terrifying!

1. Devourers
They love to eat micekings raw — no cooking necessary.

2. Steamers
They grab micekings, then fly over volcanoes so the steam and smoke make them taste good.

SIZZLE
The cook

3. Biters
Before eating micekings, they nibble them delicately to see if they like them or not.

4. Slurpers
They wrap their long tongues around micekings and slurp them up.

5. Rinsers
As soon as they catch micekings, they rinse them in a stream to wash them off.

Geronimo Stilton

MICEKINGS
THE DRAGON CROWN

Scholastic Inc.

Copyright © 2016 by Edizioni Piemme S.p.A., Palazzo Mondadori, Via Mondadori 1, 20090 Segrate, Italy. International Rights © Atlantyca S.p.A. English translation © 2018 by Atlantyca S.p.A.

The publisher does not have any control over and does not assume any responsibility for author or third-party websites or their content.

GERONIMO STILTON names, characters, and related indicia are copyright, trademark, and exclusive license of Atlantyca S.p.A. All rights reserved. The moral right of the author has been asserted. Based on an original idea by Elisabetta Dami. www.geronimostilton.com

Published by Scholastic Inc., *Publishers since 1920*, 557 Broadway, New York, NY 10012. SCHOLASTIC and associated logos are trademarks and/or registered trademarks of Scholastic Inc.

Stilton is the name of a famous English cheese. It is a registered trademark of the Stilton Cheese Makers' Association. For more information, go to www.stiltoncheese.com.

ISBN 978-1-338-21515-1

Text by Geronimo Stilton
Original title *La corona dei draganti*
Cover by Giuseppe Facciotto and Flavio Ferron
Illustrations by Giuseppe Facciotto and Alessandro Costa
Graphics by Chiara Cebraro

Special thanks to Beth Dunfey
Translated by Lidia Morson Tramontozzi
Interior design by Becky James

10 9 8 7 6 5 4 3 2 1   18 19 20 21 22

Printed in the U.S.A.   40
First printing 2018

A QUIET MORNING

It was a chilly winter morning in MOUSEBORG, the capital of Mouseking Island. The sun was just beginning to rise, and I felt incredibly mouserific!

As you know, dear reader, I love snuggling up in my cozy bed. There's nothing I enjoy more than burrowing under the **warm** blankets like a hibernating groundhog. But that morning, I wanted to feel the sun on my fur. I had to **GET OUT** in

What a fabumouse day!

the open air. So I **LEAPED** out of bed, eager as a squirrel on a nut hunt.

Oh, excuse me, I'm such a fuzzbrain! I almost forgot to introduce myself. My name is GERONIMO STILTONORD, and I'm a smarty-mouseking.

What was I squeaking about? Oh, right! That morning I woke up very early. After eating an enormouse breakfast of pancakes with reindeer butter and fjordberry JAM, I left my little hut and went looking for a peaceful spot to work.

I soon found a **bench** overlooking the fjords. Great groaning glaciers, what a lovely view. It was absomousely the perfect place to work.

I'd just pulled out all my

writing tools when someone tapped me on the tail.

It was my cousin TRAP STILTONORD, the village inventor.

"Hey there, Cousinkins! Are you ready?"

"Ready FOR WHAT?" I asked.

"You mean you don't know?" he asked

There you are . . .

Uh-oh!

with a grin. "**SVEN** decided you need some special training!"

A **CHILL** ran down my tail. "S-special . . . t-t-training?"

"Of course!" Trap said, smirking. "Haven't you heard? Real **MICEKINGS** must be in tip-top shape. We've got to be agile, athletic, and fit! And, Cuz, just look at you. You're as soft as a **SHIVERING JELLYFISH**!"

"But . . . but . . . I can't start training right now!" I stammered. "I have to prepare a new runes **lesson** for Benjamin, and then I have to write a speech for the opening of the Gloog Festival, and after that I have to copy the seventh **volume** of the *Ancient Chronicles of Micekings* . . ."

"No buts!" Trap scolded me. "You wouldn't want to disobey our **BRAVE** chief, would you?"

You have to come with me!

But . . .

My cousin had a point. When our chief, Sven, decides something, no mouseking dares disobey. If they do, he shouts

very, very, very LOUDLY!

And a bookish little mouseking like me lives for quiet.

"But I've just found the perfect place to write . . ." I moaned.

Trap **grabbed** me by the paw. "Move those paws and stop dragging that tail! Sven is waiting on the Field of Eternal Challenges."

I'M NOT A MUSCLE-MOUSEKING!

We **scurried** under the Mouseking Arch of Victory (at a run!). We *sped* through the narrow alleys behind Micekings' Helmet Museum (still at a run). Then we **SCAMPERED** through the Great Stone Square (yep, still running).

When we got to the Field of Eternal Challenges, I collapsed on a rock. I was **exhausted**!

"You look a little pale, Geronimo," Trap said. "How do you feel?"

I was too out of **breath** to answer.

"Get on your paws, you **globby jellyfish**," came a loud squeak.

I gulped. It was Sven the Shouter!

"Valiant Sven, I don't . . ." I began.

But Sven **SHOUTED** into my ear, "How many times do I have tell you that real micekings never stop?! Move those paws!

HUP, HUP, HUP!!!"

"But I . . ." I tried to explain.

"Look at you! You should train **twice** as much as the other micekings!"

"But I . . ."

"But I **NOTHING**!" bellowed Sven. "Excuses are for globby gooses! It's up to me to get you into shape for good, **SMARTY-MOUSE**." He grabbed me by the ear and **DRAGGED** me to the middle of the field.

"I have decided that THREE SPECIAL TRAINERS should instruct you!"

"B-b-but . . ." I protested. "I'm just not

It's up to me to get you into shape!

Squeak!

a **MUSCLE-MOUSEKING**!"

Before I could squeak another word, three **VERY BUFF** micekings strode toward me. They were Crusher, Smasher, and Sprainer!

"How many times can you run **around** the field without stopping?"

"How many **push-ups** can you do on one paw?"

"How many tree trunks can you lift with your whiskers?"

I shook my snout. "Er . . . actually, I . . ."

Crusher, Smasher, and Sprainer looked at

one another in despair.

"Then get going!" they exclaimed.

"Run or I'll **CRUSH** you!" cried Crusher.

"Run or I'll SMASH you!" shouted Smasher.

"Run or I'll sprain your tail!" screeched Sprainer.

My trainers forced me to . . .

Run a hundred laps around the village!

Faster!

Pant!

Do a hundred **push-ups** on one paw!

Don't stop!

Pant, pant . . .

Swim the entire length of the **ICY** fjord!

Go, go, go!

Pant, pant, pant . . .

By the time they were done with my training session, I was *totally dead on my paws*!

"*GOOD JOB*, Smarty-mouse," Sven barked. "Now it's time for your *real* training!"

My *real* training? What?! "**AAAAAARGH!!!**" I squeaked.

"On your paws, Bookmouse! What you need is **grit**," the three beefy micekings hollered.

"STRENGTH!"
"COMMITMENT!"

Oh noooo! Why does everything have to happen to me?

BEWARE OF DRAGONS!

I was looking for a quick **getaway** when I heard the sound of a horn coming from Three Lookouts Cliff.

TOOT-TOOOT TOOT-TOOOOOOT!!!

The sky was filled with **dragons** — enormouse creatures hungry for miceking meat!

Using my last breath, I shouted, **"Heeeeelp! Draaaaagons!"**

While the giant lizards swooped down on the village, the citizens of **MOUSEBORG STORMED** Copper Ironpaws's shop.

Sven barked a **SERIES** of orders at us:

13

"Don't back down, brave micekings! Everyone to the catapult! We will defend our village, my mighty Mouseborgians! **ATTAAAACK!**"

The micekings rallied. Everyone joined the attack against the dragons.

Er . . . that is, almost everyone. I was still looking for a way to **defend** myself.

"Ironpaws, is there a teensy-weensy

How about this?

sword left? A toy slingshot? Maybe an old hammer?" I begged the blacksmith.

But there was nothing. The shop was as EMPTY as a snail's shell! And, as everyone knows, my MUSCLES are pretty nonexistent. I was desperate to find something to defend myself. Anything!

I was so busy looking for a weapon that I didn't notice two dragons had come up behind me.

One was as green as mold on rotten cheese, and the other as purple as wild fjordberries. The lizards were ENORMOUSE! Stinky! And hungry!

The green dragon seized my paw in his ugly claws.

"*Sniff, sniff, sniff!* What a **SSS**weet **SSS**mell — fresh mou**SSS**eking! Let me **SSS**ample your tender meat. What a ta**SSS**ty little mor**SSS**el!"

Squeeeak! My whiskers curled up with

fear. I didn't want to become a dragon's snack!

To my relief, that oversized lizard didn't get a chance to smack his lips on me . . . because the second dragon YANKED my cape, pulling me toward him!

"Claws down, SSSpike! The mouSSSeking is mine!"

"Unh-unh, RuSSSty," growled the other. "I SSSaw him firSSSt!"

I was about to say farewell to my fur, the beautiful Thora, and the entire miceking world when a dragon the color of RED FIRE plunged down at us. It was Gobbler the Putrid, king of the dragons! He was wearing the Crown of the Seven Rubies.

"What are my earSSS hearing? SSSomeone was about to SSSample a taSSSty mouseking

19

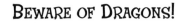

without telling hi**SSS** king?!?"

"Er . . . no, no, no. He's all your**SSS**, Your Maje**SSS**ty!" Spike mumbled.

With a shake in his snarl, Rusty said, "We ju**SSS**t wanted to make ab**SSS**olutely sure he wa**SSS**n't poi**SSS**oned!"

Gobbler licked his lips. "Come, little mou**SSS**eking. I'll ta**SSS**te you ju**SSS**t as you are!" he hissed.

On the ground next to me I **SAW** an old pot lid and a big spoon. I grabbed them and pointed them at the dragon's snout, stammering, "STAY A-AWAY, YOU U-UGLY LIZARD!"

Gobbler gave a big belly chuckle. "Thi**SSS** little mou**SSS**eking i**SSS** a cheesebrain! Perhap**SSS** I'll u**SSS**e my fiery breath to roa**SSS**t him right here, then eat him on a skewer!"

CURDLED CODFISH! This time I was

cooked, boiled, and roasted for sure.

"**HEEEEELP!!!**" I squeaked.

THE CROWN OF THE SEVEN RUBIES

Gobbler the Putrid opened his jaws wide, ready to slurp me up and **turn** me into a mouseking morsel. I **SHUT** my eyes tight when . . .

"Hey, you! You with the **ugly snout**!"

Thea and Trap were racing toward us, carrying two enormouse buckets of **WATER**. They had come to save me!

"You! What bring**SSS** you here?" Gobbler roared.

"We came to give you this!" Trap shouted.

SPLAAASHHH!! SPLAAASHHH!

Two **streams** of crystal-clear water landed on the dragon's snout. "**Nooooo! Not water!**" Gobbler growled.

You see, dragons hate clean water. It **extinguishes** their fiery breath and soaks their wings, making them too heavy to fly. Plus, when they get wet, they can catch cold. And they *hate* catching cold.

But . . . what's . . . ?

Take that!

Saved by a whisker . . .

"**Trap, Thea . . . thank you!**" I cried. My family is the best. They're always there to get me out of **trouble**.

"Scoot, you lousy lizard, or we'll soak every last scale on your overgrown body!" Thea shouted.

But **Gobbler** couldn't move. He was too busy coughing, snorting, and sniffling.

"COUGH! . . .
ARGH! . . .
PHHT!"

AAAAH-CHOOOO!

Then the king of the dragons opened his jaws, held his **breath** for a second, and . . .

"AAAAH-AAAH-AAAAAH-CHOOO!!!"

He exploded in a **thunderous** sneeze that was so loud, I saw Mount Mattress shake. The force of the sneeze **knocked** the Crown of the Seven Rubies off his head. It rolled to the ground.

"Serves you right, **YOU SLIMY, SLITHERING HEAP OF SCALES**!" Trap exclaimed.

"Shut your **SSS**nout, you chubby little mou**SSS**eking!!!" snarled Gobbler. He lurched

forward and snapped one of his sharp claws around my cousin.

"**HEEEELP!**" Trap squeaked.

I looked at my sister in alarm. "**CHEESECAKE! WHAT NOW?!**"

"Leave it to me," Thea exclaimed. "I know what to do!"

"**But, but, but** . . . the dragons have sharp claws and pointy fangs," I objected. "They want to eat us!"

We have his crown!

Thea scurried over to **PICK UP** the crown. "Now **WE** have something that belongs to them: the king's crown!"

"**Um . . . soooo?**" I mumbled.

"Don't be such a **furbrain**, Geronimo," said my sister. "It's leverage! We'll demand an exchange from Gobbler: If he gives us Trap, we'll **return** the crown."

Thea raised the crown high over her snout. "Gobbler, if you want this back, you must **RELEASE** my cousin immediately!"

"**Get your ssstinkin' pawsss off my crown!**" growled the dragon.

Before he could lift a claw, Sven gave the order to release the **catapults**. Balls of mud rained down on the surprised dragons.

"My great winged army," Gobbler roared, "**ATTAAAACK!**"

But the dragons were too busy fleeing from the mud. No one listened to Gobbler. The king of the dragons was forced to retreat.

"Thi**SSS** is not the end, you furry little gnat**SSS**! **SSS**ee you **SSS**oon!"

He flew away . . . with Trap still held tightly in his **CLAWS**!

They took Trap!

Attack now!

THE AMBASSADOR OF BEASTGARD

At last, the **dragon** attack was over.

"Micekings of **MOUSEBORG**, rejoice!" Sven the Shouter exclaimed. "We have defeated the dragons!"

"What? Did those dragons pull cheesecloth over your eyes?" Mousehilde shouted, clubbing her husband over the snout. "Didn't you notice they took our **inventor**?"

"We can't abandon Trap to the dragons' **CLUTCHES**," Thea cried.

"In that case," Sven **thundered**, "why are you all still standing around?

"A dragon **kidnapped** the inventor, right? Let's get a rescue party together and head to **BEASTGARD**!"

Squeak! What a petrifying plan! You see, Beastgard is the most DANGEROUS, **disturbing**, DREADFUL place in all of Miceking Island.

"Move those paws, SMARTY-MOUSE!" Sven told me. "Since we all know you're as spineless as a snail, I'll send some backup with you. Thea, Crusher,

Get on with it!

Let's rescue him!

We have to find Trap!

Smasher, and Sprainer will **ACCOMPANY** you."

"**BUT** . . . we can't attack the dragons in their own stronghold," I protested.

"No buts! It's an order!" Sven snorted.

"SO SAYS SVEN THE SHOUTER!"

the micekings all shouted in unison.

"B-but I . . ."

"No buts, Geronimo," Thea said. "**TRAP** needs us!"

My sister was right. We couldn't **abandon** Trap to the claws of those SCALY REPTILES! I would have to help save him no matter how terrifying that was!

No buts!

"**LOOK UP!**" Thea shouted. "What is that?"

A strange dark spot appeared in the sky. I squinted. "You mean that cloud? Wait, that can't be a cloud. It's moving too fast . . ." I trailed off.

"That's not a cloud," Thea said ominously.

"It's a **draaaagon**!" I cried.

The Mouseborgians fled in terror. But I was so scared that I stood stock-still, like a **FROZEN CODFISH**.

That was when something unexpected and absomousely incredible happened . . .

For the first time in the history of Miceking Island, the dragon did not spout **FIRE** at us.

He didn't extend his beastly **CLAWS** at us, or bare his pointy teeth at us, either. Instead, he landed peacefully on top of a large boulder.

The micekings whispered to one another,

"WHAT'S tHAt DrAGON UP tO?"

"DIDN't HE see US StANDING HErE?"

"DO YOU tHINK HE'S ON a DIEt Or SOMEtHING?"

"What are you doing here?" Sven shouted at the dragon. "Haven't you had enough?! Don't stick around our village, or we'll rip out your scales one by one!"

"Keep calm and **SSS**curry on!" the dragon bellowed. "I'm not here to roa**SSS**t you."

"Well, then, what do you want?" Sven demanded.

"My name i**sss** Gullet, and I am Bea**SSS**tgard's amba**SSS**ador," the dragon explained.

"**WHAT?!**" the micekings exclaimed.

"Our king, Gobbler the Putrid, **SSS**ent me to make an exchange," Gullet continued.

"**WHAAAAAT?!**"

"If you give me the Crown of the Seven Rubiesss, I will deliver it to King Gobbler. I promi**SSS**e to free your friend when I return to Bea**SSS**tgard."

"**WHAAAAAAAAAAAT?!**"

"**NO! NO!** And once more I shout **NO!!!**" Sven shouted. "Does

Gullet

Gullet is a dragon from the Devourer family. He is old and very wise.

Gullet has a couple of teeth missing and he has become very lazy. Nonetheless, Gobbler named him Beastgard's ambassador because he has always been loyal to the king.

I'm so sleepy!

Gobbler think we're nothing but a bunch of foolish furbrains? Why should we believe you?"

With a **CHILLING** whirling of wings, Gullet roared, "You don't tru**SSS**t me, pe**SSS**t? Why, I could **fry** you in a **SSS**econd! If I wanted to eat you, I would have done it already."

But Sven refused to be intimidated. "If you want Gobbler's **crown** back, you must agree to our terms."

"Ju**SSS**t what would those term**SSS** be?" the dragon demanded.

"Our miceking heroes will take the crown to Beastgard. That's where the exchange will take place," Sven announced. ***"TAKE IT OR LEAVE IT!"***

Gullet extended his paw. "Deal! I am an honorable dragon. I keep my word!"

And so the pact was sealed.

"This **GREAT** journey will require a means of transport," Sven thundered.

Everyone turned to Aurigard, driver of the most famouse taxicart in Mouseborg (probably because it's the only one!).

"Where do you want to go? How long are you staying? Show me your **gold**!" he **DEMANDED**.

"Aurigard, this is an **emergency** . . . no, a cat-astrophe! No gold!" Sven growled.

Let's go!

Aurigard sighed. "Fine! But you better return my taxicart without a single SCRATCH."

"**SMARTY-MOUSE**, you better take good care of that taxicart!" Sven bellowed at me.

Watch Your Fur, Geronimo!

Before we left, we filled the cart with everything we needed for our expedition. Thea was in charge of the equipment. She loaded the taxicart with:

➤ **seven** iron hammers
➤ **ten** miceking shields
➤ **twenty** goat-wool blankets
➤ **fifty** miceking tails of rope

Then Crusher, Smasher, and Sprainer added these provisions:

Iron
hammers

Miceking
shields

Goat-wool
blankets

Lots of rope

THREE gigantic wheels of Stenchberg cheese

SIX berry-jam tarts

TWENTY jars of chestnut honey

FORTY smoked-herring sandwiches

WHAT A MOUNTAIN OF MOUSERIFIC FOOD!

"At least we don't have to carry all this stuff in our packs." I sighed.

"You're right, Geronimo," Thea agreed. "We are very **lucky**! And it's all thanks to you . . . because you'll be pulling the taxicart."

"**Whaaaat?** Why me?!" I screeched.

Gigantic wheels of Stenchberg cheese

Berry-jam tarts

Chestnut honey jars

Smoked-herring sandwiches

Crusher, Smasher, and Sprainer barked,
"Don't complain, **SMARTY-MOUSE!**"
"We have other work to do!"
"We've got to keep an eye on the **dragon**! You can't trust him!"

"Hey!" Gullet snarled. "I'm a **SSS**erious amba**SSS**ador, I **SSS**wear!" He turned and raised his wings toward Beastgard. "Follow me, miceking**SSS**!"

And so we set out on our journey. After many weary hours, we reached the Hills of Wisewords.

Are you okay, Gerry Berry?

I'm coming, I'm coming ... pant, pant ...

Crusher, Smasher, and Sprainer skipped along the slope, spry as mountain goats, while I DRAGGED the cart behind me, slow as a sloth.

"Hurry up, GERONIMO!" Thea urged me.

Puff...

What a pleasant stroll!

Hup, hup, hup...

Yeah!

"Check out that ratastic view! Feel that BR☼ISK, clean air!"

But I was too tired. Exhausted. Beat!!!

Truth be told, I wasn't the only one. Gullet was flying very low, huffing and puffing little clouds of smoke .

"Puff, puff . . . I'm not uSSSed to so much flying BACK and FORTH without a SSSnack!" the dragon moaned. He stared longingly at the taxicart.

I was instantly suspicious. "You're not thinking of —"

But I didn't get a chance to finish squeaking. Gullet stopped flapping his wings and . . .

BAAANG!

He landed RIGHT SMACK into the middle of taxicart!

44

"Ahhhh!! I think I'll catch a few **Z𝘚𝘚𝘚**," he hissed, making himself comfortable.

The cart couldn't take Gullet's great weight. It creaked and got stuck. The wheels **SPUN** around and . . .

The cart sped *down, down, down* the slope, *DRAGGING* me along with it! We dodged a tree, grazed a couple of sharp rocks, and zipped across a stretch of thorny bushes.

In spite of the bumpy ride, Gullet fell fast asleep.

Suddenly, a **DEEP** crevice yawned before us.

"Wake up, Gullet!" I cried. "Help! We're **faaaaalling**!"

But the dragon had drifted into a deep, deep sleep.

I clung to the cart like a mussel on a reef until . . .

SCREEEEECH!!!

Crusher, Smasher, and Sprainer stopped the taxicart just in the nick of time. We teetered at the edge of the gorge . . . but we were safe!

Zzzzz!
Zzzzz!
Zzzzz!

Saved by a whisker . . .

A Ghastly Night

After that miserable **misadventure**, we stopped to take a rest. The **sun** was hiding behind black clouds in the distance. Snowflakes as big as cheese puffs steadily fell to the ground. The icy north wind began to blow. It was so cold . . . **Brrrr!**

Crusher, Smasher, and Sprainer looked **around**.

"This doesn't look like a very good place to spend the night . . ."

"Not much shelter, plus it *SLOPES* too much . . ."

"We'll find a better spot!"

But the mere thought of moving made me groan. **"Noooo! I can't take another step!!!"**

Luckily, Thea had spotted something. "There's a cave down there," she said. "Let's take a look."

But the cave was **VERY** dark, **VERRRY** damp, and **VERRRY**, **VERRRRRYYYYY** deep.

"What if there's a b-bear in there?" I stammered. "Or vampire bats? Or the Abominable Snow D-dragon?"

"A snow **dragon**?

A Snow Dragon?!

"Don't be such a 'fraidy mouseking, Geronimo!" Thea snorted. Crusher, Smasher, and Sprainer peeked inside the **CAVE**.

"Interesting," Crusher commented.

Oooh!

What is it?

"**WHAT DO YOU SEE?**" I asked, shivering.

"Incredible," Smasher replied.

"WHAT'S IN THERE?" I repeated.

"Impressive!" Sprainer exclaimed.

"**STINKY STENCHBERG**, just tell us **WHAT** you see!" I blurted.

Crusher shrugged. "Nothing. It's so **DARK** we can't see past the tips of our snouts."

"Oh, enough already," squeaked Thea. "Do you want to stay out here freezing your tails off? Let's go in!"

We went in. By that time, we were soaked to the fur and frozen like icicles. Gullet was the only one who didn't join us. But that was fine with me, because no mouseking wants to snooze next to a dragon!

As soon as I closed my EYES, a sound like thunder made me spring back to my paws.

SNORRRRRE! SNORRRRRRE!

Crusher, Smasher, and Sprainer yelled, "Stop that or I'll CRUSH you, Geronimo!"

"Stop that or I'll **SMASH** you, Geronimo!"

"Stop that or I'll **sprain** your tail, Geronimo!"

"But . . . but . . . but . . . it's not me!" I **PROTESTED**.

It was Gullet. And his snores were louder than an **erupting** volcano!

We tried everything we could think of to make the sound stop. We tried whistling at Gullet. We tried tossing pebbles at his tail, but they just bounced off. We tried putting our snouts under our cloaks and our 🐾🐾🐾🐾 over our ears.

But nothing worked. It was a ghastly night!

The next morning, we woke up to find the entrance to the **CAVE** blocked by a thick, dense wall of snow.

"**WE'RE TRAPPED!**" I moaned.

Crusher, Smasher, and Sprainer tried to push, pick, and dig through the snow with their **super-strong** paws, but it was all in vain.

Just when I thought we were doomed . . .

The ice began to **MELT**! Moldy mozzarella! But how? It was still as cold as a glacier inside the cave.

"Move a**SSS**ide if you don't want your fur **SSS**inged!"

It was Gullet. With a powerful burst of fiery breath, he **MELTED** the wall of snow and unblocked the cave's entrance.

Sizzling Stenchberg slices, I was sh**o**cked. I never thought I'd live to see the day I'd be saved by a **dragon**!

THE CHARGE OF THE
BEARDED BILLY GOAT

We continued on our journey. We MARCHED and MARCHED and MARCHED some more. We trudged so far I was sure my paws would shrivel up and fall off!

A terrible snowstorm hit us at full force at the foot of Mount Mattress. To keep my tail from freezing, I put on:

Brrr . . . I'm freezing!

- **ONE** pair of leather earmuffs
- **TWO** woolen blankets
- **THREE** fur coats
- **FOUR** pairs of super-heavy socks
- **SALTY SARDINES!** I was

so bundled up, I could barely move my paws.

Our **path** came to an end at the edge of a ravine. The only way across was a narrow **STONE** bridge. The others **scurried** over, but I hesitated.

"Come on!" Crusher shouted at me. "Don't be such a **clam**!"

I-I'll try . . .

"Don't be a 'fraidy mouseking, Geronimo. Just do it!" snorted Thea.

The bridge was very skinny, barely wide enough to fit the TAXICART. I sighed and took a nervous step forward.

"I-I'm coming . . ." I called.

Squeak! My whiskers trembled with

You can do it!

Come on, Ger!

Move those paws!

fear, my **PAWS** wobbled like melted cheese, and my snout spun around in circles. You see, I am absomousely terrified of heights!

When I reached the other side, I collapsed on the ground. "Thank goodmouse it's over," I wailed.

But this was just the beginning. As our journey continued, we had to:

• Climb the **STEEP** Peak Pantsalot, where I slipped and hung by my tail like a worm on a fishing line!

Ooops!

• Cross the TREACHEROUS Frozen Lake. It was *SOOO* slippery, *SOOO* incredibly slippery, *SOOOOO* enormousely slippery that I stumbled and hit my snout ten times!

• Hike the Plain of Storms, where hailstones as big as mozzarellas pelted us!

• Shimmy down the plateau in the middle of an earthquake!

AAAAAAAAHHHHHHHHHHHHHH!

When I felt the earth move under my

Yee-ouch!

THE BILLY GOAT

The billy goat is a peaceful, sleepy mountain goat. But whatever you do, don't startle it — it becomes extremely unpredictable when it's alarmed!

FUN FACTS:

· The billy goat has soft white fur and a handsome goatee.
· The herd lives on Peak Pantsalot because the valley is too hot for all that fur!

paws, I turned PALER than a cold codfish. "Ummm . . . why is the ground shaking?"

"Oh, it's probably just a small AVALANCHE," Thea tried to reassure me.

SUDDENLY, a cloud of rocks and snow billowed behind us. From the rocky ridge emerged a . . . BILLY GOAT!

ANOTHER appeared . . . and then ANOTHER . . . and then ANOTHER . . . and about a hundred more.

"They're **heading** right for us," I squeaked.

"The noise frightened them," squeaked Thea. "QUICK. FIND A PLACE TO HIDE!"

I scurried to do as she said. You see, my sister has a special ability to communicate with animals LARGE and small. As she whispered soothingly to the billy goats, the rest of us scampered behind the CART.

I curled up like a ball of cheese, trying to make myself as small as possible, when . . .

BOINK!

Something bounced off my snout.

"HEEELP!!" I cried, leaping into Crusher's paws. "They're attacking us!"

"Galloping goatherds! Get down!" he bellowed.

61

"Can't you see it's only . . ." Smasher began.

"**A GOAT KID?**" Sprainer concluded.

Sure enough, it was just a little billy goat. It wagged its tail at me.

Flaming fjordberries, I looked like such a cheesebrain!

Are you seriously afraid of a teensy-tiny goat kid?!

Ohhhh . . . it's just a kid?

Thea had **calmed** the herd, so we took the little kid back to his mom.

Just when I had (almost) gotten used to all the unexpected ups and downs of our expedition, Thea called, "Look down there!"

"It's an ice swamp!" exclaimed Crusher.

"There's a geyser*!" Smasher continued.

"Check out that enormouse VOLCANO!" finished Sprainer.

My sister nodded. "That means . . ."

Gullet swooped down in front of us, bellowing,

"WELCOME TO THE LAND OF THE DRAGONS!!!"

*Geyser: A hot spring that intermittently shoots out bursts of water.

THE LAND OF THE DRAGONS

The Land of the Dragons is a **dreadful**, **GHASTLY**, **HORRIFIC** place where no mouseking should ever, ever set paw. I looked around and shivered. The frozen ground trembled beneath my paws. Puffs of dark smoke rose from the ground. Rivers of **fluorescent** lava flowed all around us.

"Ahhh! What a refre**SSS**hing breeze!" Gullet boomed.

"Actually, it's the **stench of rotten eggs**," I whispered to Thea.

We left the taxicart safely

behind a rock and **followed** Gullet into a tunnel that plunged down, down, down into a deep pit. It was **DARKER** than the inside of a dragon's jaws.

"This heat is unbearable!" I complained.

"I'm **MELTING**!" said Crusher.

"I'm **dissolving**!" added Smasher.

"I'm **liquefying**!" cried Sprainer.

A deep voice suddenly croaked,

"**Sss**top right there, my delectable little mor**sss**el**sss**!"

Leaping lizards! From the shadows of the tunnel emerged the most menacing, massive dragon I'd ever seen!

Slowly, very **slowly**, one . . . no, two . . . no, **ten** dragons stepped forward. When

I spotted their sharp CLAWS, I began to tremble like Parmesan pudding.

"Gullet, how thoughtful of you! You brought uSSS SSSome SSScrumptious miceking SSSnackSSS!"

My whiskers twisted themselves into knots. **Squeeeeak!**

But Gullet just laughed. "**HA, HA, HA**, you wish! The**sss**e miceking**sss** are not for you!"

"No **sss**nack**sss** for u**sss**? Not even a nibble?" one dragon **complained**. "I'll bet

We want the micekings!

Don't even think about it!

you didn't bring u**SSS** any H⊙+ pepper**SSS**, either."

Gullet puffed his chest. "Perhap**SSS** you are not aware that I am a dragon on a mission!"

"Who care**SSS**! We want to eat the**SSS**e **SSS**weet little miceking**SSS**!"

Gullet **SHIELDED** us with his scaly body. "The**SSS**e miceking**SSS** are not to be touched! They're for our king, Gobbler the Putrid!"

"Gobbler is no longer our king," the other dragon declared.

"What did you **SSS**ay?!" boomed Gullet.

Wait, what? Gobbler was the king of the dragons, wasn't he? **I was so confused!**

"Enough, you lousy lizard snouts!" Thea snapped. "Stop wasting time. We have to rescue TRAP!"

I may have mentioned this earlier, but my sister, Thea, is the most COURAGEOUS mouseking I know.

But the dragons weren't listening. They began arguing among themselves. Their roars boomed so noisily, the cave walls shook!

"Finally, fresssh meat to eat in one big chomp!"

Let us through!

Hunhhh?

"But I want to **SSS**tew them fir**SSS**t!"

"Put your claw**SSS** down! The**SSS**e miceking**SSS** are mine!"

We quickly took advantage of the dragons' bickering to make our *GETAWAY*. And that's how we made it to the Pit of Fiery Breath, the center of **Beastgard**, the terrifying capital of the Land of the Dragons!

A King without His Crown

Gullet pointed to a **wide** space at the center of the pit.

"We are here at la**SSS**t, little miceking**SSS**! Before u**SSS** i**SSS** the Bea**SSS**tgard A**SSS**embly **SSS**quare!"

Down in the pit were **HUNDREDS** of dragons. At the center, we spotted **Gobbler the Putrid**! I couldn't take my eyes off all those scaly wings, open jaws, and SHARP claws.

"Help! Take me home, Thea! I told you I didn't want to come!" I squeaked in terror.

There was a little dragon guard PERCHED on a flagpole.

"AHHK! AHHK! AHHK!

SSSpike and RuSSSty have something to SSSay!" he croaked.

Gobbler strode forward MENACINGLY. "What do you want, lizard SSSnouts?"

"We want to know why you get to be king!" Spike shouted.

"That'SSS right! You no longer poSSSeSSS the crown!" the other dragons cried.

"Who do you think should be king?" Gobbler snapped.

"Well, um . . . how about Russsty? He'SSS SSStrong!"

"How about SSSPIKE?" added another. "He haSSS an aweSSSome fiery SSSpurt!"

Gobbler was getting annoyed at all the racket. "If any of you wish to be KING, you have to challenge me, and then you have

I'm always right!

RUSTY

Spike and Rusty are two young dragons, friends to the scale. They are arrogant and obnoxious. They're always finding something to complain about, and they never miss a chance to get into trouble.

SPIKE

I'm strongest!

to beat me. That's the rule! **SSS**o bring it on! **SSS**tep forward!" he growled.

"I'll challenge you to a conte**SSS**t of strength at Iron Tail!" Spike shouted.

"And I'll challenge you to **SSS**ee which of u**SSS** can make the longe**SSS**t fire-breathing *BLAZE*!" cried Rusty.

Wait! Were the dragons challenging their own KING?

"Don't you get it,

Geronimo? The dragons don't recognize Gobbler as their king because he lost his **crown**," explained Thea.

As usual, my sister had struck the cheese on the curd. Gobbler had to have that crown if he wanted to be king! That's why he was so determined to get it **BACK**.

"Bring it on," thundered Gobbler. "Let the challenge begin!"

That was Gullet's cue. He took off, croaking, "**Ssstinky mud ssswamps!** Gobbler need**sss** my help. **SSS**tay where you are. I'll be right back!"

"**NO, NO, NO!** Where are you going! Don't leave us!" I squeaked.

But Gullet was already gone. And we were all alone with a swarm of **RAVENOUS** dragons just a few tails away!

I had a **BAD** feeling about this . . .

"This is **terrible**. Wh-what are we g-going to do now?" I stammered.

Luckily, Thea had already thought of a plan. "Let's find Trap!"

RUN, GERONIMO!

I was about to follow my sister when a **SHARP** claw tapped me on the shoulder. A huge dragon as red as fire breathed down on me.

"What a **SSSucculent SSSurprisSSe** . . . Fresh meat for my **sssnack**!"

"I w-warn you, I'm n-not at all t-tasty!" I stammered. "You can roast me or boil me, but either way, I'm as tough as a hunk of moldy mozzarella!"

"Well in that case, I'll eat you . . . **RAW**!"

Fortunately, Crusher, Smasher, and Sprainer grabbed me by the paw, squeaking, "Run, GERONIMO!"

We scurried away from that hungry dragon

as fast as our paws could carry us, but he was right on our tail. A trickle of drool spilled from his open jaws, leaving a gooey trail behind him.

"Oh, I SSSee, you want to play hide and SSSeek. That'SSS fine with me! I'll find you!" the dragon hollered.

First, we hid inside a barrel in the Salty Sand Grotto. 1 But the dragon was quick to find us. Before we knew it, we were on the run again . . . and

1

Out of the way!

now our clothes were on fire! All it took was one breath, and he'd almost incinerated us.

Achoo! Achoo! Achoo!

Next, we hid in **Parched Pepper Cavern**. [2] We tried concealing ourselves behind a mountain of pepper . . . but soon we began to *SNEEZE*, and the dragon found us again!

After that, we hid in the **SILO OF SPICES**. [3] We crawled inside a chest of supersmelly red peppers.

Come in here!

"Trust me, he won't find us here. Quickly, everybody in!"

My sister was right. The dragon was so distracted by the smell of his favorite hot peppers that he didn't detect our scent. After a few minutes, he started looking for us elsewhere.

I breathed a big sigh of relief. We were safe at last.

But not for long! Suddenly, the lid to the chest lifted. A dark shadow hovered over us. And then we heard a gigantic green dragon snorting,

"SSSNIFF! SSSNIFF! SSSNIFFF! SSSNIFF! SSSNIFF! SSSNIFFF! SSSNIFF! SSSNIFF! SSSNIFFF!

"A real chef can **SSS**niff out miceking**SSS** from five cavern**SSS** away!"

Crunchy cheddar chunks! It was **Sizzle**, the court's cook.

This time we were truly **TRAPPED**!

SIZZLE THE COOK

Sizzle is the cook for not just the king but for all the dragons. He uses his gigantic soup spoon to whack hungry dragons when they get unruly. His domain is the infamouse Dragon Kitchen, where he prepares lip-smacking dishes made from fresh miceking meat.

Miceking stew for everybody!

TONIGHT'SSS DINNER: MICEKING SSSTEW!

The Dragon Kitchen was a **LARGE** cave filled to the ceiling with sacks of potatoes, mountains of onions, and mounds of braided **stinky garlic**.

Sizzle put down the chest we were being held in. "Five rodent**SSS**! This will be a deliciou**SSS** banquet!" He began **TAPPING** each of us on the snout with his spoon. He started with Crusher, then Smasher, and then Sprainer.

TAP, TAP, TAP!

"The**SSS**e three have too much mu**SSS**cle. Better **SSS**low cook them," he muttered.

Then it was my sister's turn.
TAP, TAP, TAP!

"Mmm, tender miceking meat, excellent with bean**SSS** and oil!"

Finally, it was my turn. **TAP, TAP, TAP!**

"Oooh!! Not too tough, not too tender. Thi**SSS** one i**SSS** perfect for miceking **SSS**tew!"

Ouch!   Excellent!

I shuddered. What a **dreadful** way to end my brief life!

Sizzle threw a bunch of celery, tomatoes, and beets into an enormouse **POT** of boiling water.

Then he used my own tail to tie me up like a sausage, humming . . .

"La la la la lalalala . . . lalalalala lalalala . . . A brushing of oil here . . ." 1

Squeeeak! That tickled!

"A **SSS**prinkling of flour there . . ." 2

Squeeeak! That itched!

"And a pinch of **SSS**pice here!" 3

Squeeeak! That burned!

"I don't want to be the main ingredient in miceking stew!" I wailed.

Sizzle ignored me. "On the count of three, I'll to**SSS** you in. Ready?"

"**HEEEELP!**" I screamed.

At that moment, Crusher, Smasher, and Sprainer burst out of the **chest**.

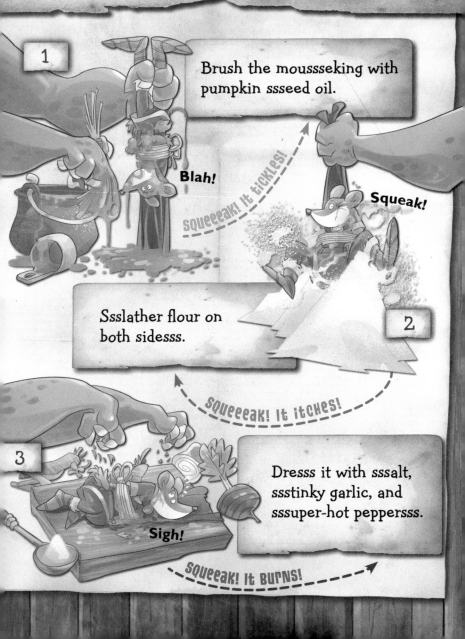

Surprised, Sizzle bellowed, "Get back in there, fuzz ball**SSS**!"

FASTER than the smell of simmering stew, Smasher snatched the spoon from Sizzle's apron and began **POUNDING** it on the pots.

"Pa**SSS** that back to me right now!" Sizzle shouted.

Instead, Smasher threw the wooden **spoon** to Crusher, who threw it to Sprainer,

Perrrrrfect throw!!!

BANG! BOINK!
CRASH!

who **THREW** it back to Smasher.

Got it!

Now Sizzle was **madder** than a mussel in a mouseking's net. He chased the three brawny micekings all around the kitchen.

"**SSS**top!! Pa**SSS** that back! Pa**SSS** it back!!"

But the three MICEKINGS were *speedier* than swordfish in the spring. As Sizzle tried to catch them, he bumped into the sideboard. It teetered, shook, and fell to the ground with a loud smash.

CRAAASH!

All (and I do mean *all*!) the jars of garlic, mustard, and pickles rolled to the floor.

"You'll pay for thi**SSS**, you pe**SSS**ky rodent**SSS**!" cried Sizzle. But before he could lift a claw, he slipped on a drop of oil. He desperately tried to balance himself on the table edge, but it was too late. He crashed to the ground with a thunderous racket.

At that moment, another dragon stomped into the Dragon Kitchen. It was Gullet!

"**SSS**izzle, you two-faced carnivorou**SSS** klutz! What in the name of Bea**SSS**tgard are you doing?!" growled the ambassador.

The cook stared longingly at us. "The**SSS**e are my miceking**SSS**! I found them and I'll cook them the way I want to. Under**SSS**tand?!"

"No!" bellowed Gullet, grinding his

SHARP teeth. "Let them go. Now! Or I'll roa**SSS**t you like a che**SSS**tnut!"

"**SSS**ure, have it your way!" the court's cook snorted. "But then don't complain when I **SSS**erve stinky **Beet** **sss**oup for dinner for the next two week**SSS**!"

ESCAPE FROM BEASTGARD

We scampered after Gullet, who led us to Gobbler's private chamber. It was an enormouse cave with a private pool of fetid water and a canopy bed made of little bones. **What a ghastly place!**

Gobbler was waiting for us with his claws crossed. Trap was wound up tight inside his scaly, mega-long tail.

"Geronimo! Thea!" my cousin squeaked. "You came to rescue me!"

"Shush!" snorted the king of the dragons. "Or do you want me to make you into miceking caSSSerole?"

"Take your claws off my cousin, you

wretched reptile! Aren't you a dragon of your word?" Thea replied.

Gobbler almost incinerated her with his fiery **EYES**. Then he hissed, "I will free the rodent, but fir**sss**t give me the crown!"

Thea had kept the **crown** safely hidden throughout our entire journey. She waited for

I'm fr

Finally!

Gobbler to push Trap toward us, and then she finally rolled the crown to him.

"You're free, Cousin!" I squeaked, my eyes brimming with **tears**.

Trap ran to **hug** us.

"I knew I could count on you!!! *My family is awesome!*" he squeaked.

We were still hugging when we heard someone outside. It was Rusty and Spike!

"Gobbler, oh Gobbler? Where are you hiding?" they rasped.

"The dragon**SSS**' challenge i**SSS** not over!"

"Are your scale**SSS** shaking with fear?"

"**SSSTINKY SSSEWER BREATH!** I'll show you who'**SSS** king of the dragon**SSS** . . ." Gobbler snarled.

Before he stomped out, I asked, "How do we get out of Beastgard?"

Gobbler snickered. "Our deal was to trade the crown for your cousin. We didn't **SSS**ay anything about helping you **ESSSCAPE**. Am I right, Gullet?"

"Ab**SSS**olutely!" snorted Gullet.

"I **SSS**ugge**SSS**t you **SSS**curry away before we make you into miceking **SSS**tew!" Gobbler continued.

Thea, Trap, and I **LOOKED** at one another in despair. How would we ever make it out of Beastgard without losing our fur?

But Thea had an idea. "We can get out the same way we came in. **Let's move our tails!**"

And so we left the **dragons** bickering among themselves. We scurried quietly through the fountains of sulfur . . .

FESTERING FJORD FILLETS!

My whiskers were trembling in terror!

Fortunately, **Gobbler** was too busy showing the rebellious dragons who was boss to waste any time on us.

"As punishment, you will write: **GOBBLER ISSS OUR KING EVEN WITHOUT A CROWN**! Fifty time**SSS**! Each!

"I **SSS**aid fifty time**SSS**, not one le**SSS**! Do

you under**sss**tand? And don't think you can get out of it ju**sss**t becau**sss**e you can't count!"

The dragons around him hissed,

"We await your ordersss, great Gobbler!"

"Thisss wasss all jussst a big missstake!"

"Forgive usss, oh great Gobbler the Putrid!"

It was the perfect time for our getaway.

"Follow me!" Thea whispered. **"NOW!"**

We slipped behind them and circled back to the Pit of Fiery Breath, where we'd left the taxicart. I was afraid the guard dragons would **BREAK** every one of our bones, but . . .

SNORE . . . SNORE . . . SNORE!

They were sound asleep . . . and snoring louder than hibernating cave bears!

"Shhhhh!" Trap whispered. "If we walk on our tippy-**PAWS**, they won't hear us!"

I was slipping along softly, my ears quivering with fear, when suddenly something grabbed me by the tail. It was a

Good thing she's sleeping . . .

Ssslurp!

dragon! She caught me in her claws as she **slept**. She sniffed me, stroked my fur, and gave me a **SLOBBERY** kiss.

"Help me!" I whispered as I tried to free myself from her clutches.

The dragon, still asleep, was about to **nibble** at my ear when Crusher, Smasher, and Sprainer snapped me from her **CLAWS**. I let out a big sigh of relief.

"You thought you were a goner, didn't you, Cuz?" TRAP chuckled.

After a long trek, we finally reached the taxicart.

"There it is!" I squeaked. "Let's scram!"

"We better **haul tail**," Thea agreed. "Soon it'll be dinnertime for the dragons. There's no time to lose!"

A Cat-astrophic Crash!

Our **MISSION** was over, and I couldn't wait to get home. But . . . SQUEEAK!! The long, treacherous **climb** over Mount Mattress still lay ahead of us.

One, two. One, two . . .

I was ready to **CROAK** with

Pant, pant, pant . . .

exhaustion. Meanwhile, Trap was sprawled across the cart with his paws in the air.

"I'll help you, Cuz. One, two. One, two. One, two! Follow the beat!" he muttered.

"Huff . . ." I panted. "Could we stop . . . huff, huff, huff . . . for a second?"

But the three muscular micekings just laughed. "Are you serious?! Don't be such a measly little mollusk! You've got to get rid of that tummy! Work those muscles! Prove you're a real mouseking, like us!"

I was about to answer, when suddenly . . .

BA-AA-AA-AAA!
BA-A-A-AAAA!

Thea smiled. "It's the little billy goat we met on our way here."

Trap jumped off the CART and went to

pet him. "Aw, he's so cute!

"Gerrykins, he seems **veeeery** happy to see you again."

My cousin was right. The **KID** covered me with wet kisses.

"I'm happy to see you, too, but I can't stay," I said, smiling.

But the kid wouldn't let go of me. So I took my paw off the taxicart for just a microsecond and . . .

Uh-oh . . . stop!

The cart slid down, down, down the hill!

STINKING STENCHBERG!

I had to stop it before . . .

CRASH!

Too late. The cart smashed into a tree and **BROKE** into a million pieces.

SRAAACK!

Oh no, what a mess!

A CAT-ASTROPHIC CRASH!

I **LOOKED** at what was left of the cart. Alas, it was almost nothing.

Crusher, Smasher, and Sprainer chuckled. "Now you're a **GONER**, smarty-mouse!"

"Aurigard and Sven are going to make **miceking meatballs** out of you!"

"**TOO BAD**. Just when we were actually starting to like you . . ."

Anxiously, I wrung my paws.

"Well, Cuz, this is your lucky day. It so happens I'm the most famouse **inventor** in Mouseborg," declared Trap. "I have the perfect solution to your problem: **RESINGLUE**!"

"Uhh . . . are you sure it'll work?" I asked. You see, every time Trap invents something new, he insists on testing it on me. Unfortunately, his inventions almost never work!

RESINGLUE

Resinglue is a super-gluey substance made of pine needles left to ferment in the sun for three weeks. Then the fermented pine needles are mixed with the resin taken from tree bark. It glues everything and is super-strong. So be careful not to paste your paws together!

Trap **TOOK** a small jar out of his pocket. "Positive! My latest INVENTION will fix this cart so well Aurigard won't notice a thing."

"Um . . . are you very, very SURE?" I asked.

SURE? SURE? SURE? SURE? SURE?

"Of course," TRAP answered, slapping me on the tail. "Let's get to work."

It was painstakingly boring work, but we did it. And in the end, I had to admit my cousin was right. The taxicart looked like new.

STOP! WHERE'S MY TAXICART?

When we finally got back to MOUSEBORG, we were received as heroes. Sven the Shouter was waiting for us in the Great Stone Square. He was positively bursting with **pride**. With him stood Mousehilde and their daughter, **Thora**. (Ah, Thora is so beautiful!) All the micekings in the village were lined up behind them.

"Micekings of Mouseborg," Sven shouted, "I am happy to announce that Trap the **inventor** is back home with his tail still intact!"

Everyone cheered with joy and SHOUTED our names.

"HURRAY FOR THE INVENTOR!"
"HURRAY FOR THE THREE STRONG MICEKINGS!"
"HURRAY FOR THEA AND GERONIMO!"

"To honor these micekings for having defeated the dragons in their own land, I will reward them with the highest honor: the **MICEKING HELMET**!" Sven shouted.

"SO SAYS SVEN THE SHOUTER!"

everyone cheered.

I couldn't believe my ears. I was about to receive my very first miceking helmet!

"Here I am, VALIANT Sven," I squeaked.

But no sooner did Sven raise the helmet than a scream shattered my eardrums.

"EVERYONE STOP! Where's my taxicart?"

Oh no! It was Aurigard. And he was

looking at me menacingly. My whiskers began quivering like a bowl full of gloog.

Aurigard strode toward me. "Did you take **very**, **very**, **very** good care of my taxicart, Geronimo?"

"I, yes. I mean . . ." I stammered. "Just a little scratch, or maybe two . . ."

1

Hmmm . . .

Aurigard checked his taxicart millitail by millitail, grumbling, "Huh! There's dust on the wheels . . . and a little SCRATCH here . . ." **1**

The closer he came to the cart, the more my whiskers trembled!

Finally, he was satisfied. **2** "I knew my taxicart was nice and **STURDY**!"

As he squeaked, he leaned on the side of the cart and . . . CREEEEEAK!

2

Just a little scratch, that's all.

CREEEE

A **CRACK** began to appear. Then another. And another until . . .

CRAAACK! The taxicart disintegrated into a thousand pieces! **3**

"Wh-whaaaat!" sputtered Aurigard angrily.

I shrank inside my fur, trying to **disappear**. "Um . . . well, there was this one tiny problem . . ."

But Sven's shout made me **quake** with fear from the tip of my whiskers to the tip of my tail.

"Geronimo, did you honestly think you could get away with this? No helmet for you!" Sven shouted.

"But . . . but . . . I . . ." I tried to protest.

"Shut your snout!" he thundered. "Now we will celebrate with a BANQUET of plenty. Gloog for everyone! But not you, Geronimo. Before you join the feast, you must FIX the taxicart."

I sighed. There was nothing to do but settle myself into a corner and begin rebuilding. I started patching the taxicart together piece by piece.

Fortunately for me, miceking banquets last a veeeeeery long time. When I finished, I joined my friends at the feast. Gloog had never tasted better to this hungry mouseking!

Would I ever earn a MiceKiNG HeLMet? Who knows? Maybe one day I would . . .

BUT THAT'S ANOTHER MICEKING STORY FOR ANOTHER DAY!

Don't miss any adventures of the Micekings!

#1 Attack of the Dragons

#2 The Famouse Fjord Race

#3 Pull the Dragon's Tooth!

#4 Stay Strong, Geronimo!

#5 The Mysterious Message

#6 The Helmet Holdup

#7 The Dragon Crown

Be sure to read all my fabumouse adventures!

#1 Lost Treasure of the Emerald Eye

#2 The Curse of the Cheese Pyramid

#3 Cat and Mouse in a Haunted House

#4 I'm Too Fond of My Fur!

#5 Four Mice Deep in the Jungle

#6 Paws Off, Cheddarface!

#7 Red Pizzas for a Blue Count

#8 Attack of the Bandit Cats

#9 A Fabumouse Vacation for Geronimo

#10 All Because of a Cup of Coffee

#11 It's Halloween, You 'Fraidy Mouse!

#12 Merry Christmas, Geronimo!

#13 The Phantom of the Subway

#14 The Temple of the Ruby of Fire

#15 The Mona Mousa Code

#16 A Cheese-Colored Camper

#17 Watch Your Whiskers, Stilton!

#18 Shipwreck on the Pirate Islands

#19 My Name Is Stilton, Geronimo Stilton

#20 Surf's Up, Geronimo!

#21 The Wild, Wild West

#22 The Secret of Cacklefur Castle

A Christmas Tale

#23 Valentine's Day Disaster

#24 Field Trip to Niagara Falls

#25 The Search for Sunken Treasure

#26 The Mummy with No Name

#27 The Christmas Toy Factory

#28 Wedding Crasher

#29 Down and Out Down Under

#30 The Mouse Island Marathon

#31 The Mysterious Cheese Thief

Christmas Catastrophe

#32 Valley of the Giant Skeletons

#33 Geronimo and the Gold Medal Mystery

#34 Geronimo Stilton, Secret Agent

#35 A Very Merry Christmas

#36 Geronimo's Valentine

#37 The Race Across America

#38 A Fabumouse School Adventure

#39 Singing Sensation

#40 The Karate Mouse

#41 Mighty Mount Kilimanjaro

#42 The Peculiar Pumpkin Thief

#43 I'm Not a Supermouse!

#44 The Giant Diamond Robbery

#45 Save the White Whale!

#46 The Haunted Castle

#47 Run for the Hills, Geronimo!

#48 The Mystery in Venice

#49 The Way of the Samurai

#50 This Hotel Is Haunted!

#51 The Enormouse Pearl Heist

#52 Mouse in Space!

#53 Rumble in the Jungle

#54 Get into Gear, Stilton!

#55 The Golden Statue Plot

#56 Flight of the Red Bandit

#57 The Stinky Cheese Vacation

#58 The Super Chef Contest

#59 Welcome to Moldy Manor

#60 The Treasure of Easter Island

#61 Mouse House Hunter

#62 Mouse Overboard!

#63 The Cheese Experiment

#64 Magical Mission

#65 Bollywood Burglary

#66 Operation: Secret Recipe

#67 The Chocolate Chase

#68 Cyber-Thief Showdown

Up Next!

#69 Hug a Tree, Geronimo

Don't miss any of my special edition adventures!

THE KINGDOM OF FANTASY

THE QUEST FOR PARADISE:
THE RETURN TO THE KINGDOM OF FANTASY

THE AMAZING VOYAGE:
THE THIRD ADVENTURE IN THE KINGDOM OF FANTASY

THE DRAGON PROPHECY:
THE FOURTH ADVENTURE IN THE KINGDOM OF FANTASY

THE VOLCANO OF FIRE:
THE FIFTH ADVENTURE IN THE KINGDOM OF FANTASY

THE SEARCH FOR TREASURE:
THE SIXTH ADVENTURE IN THE KINGDOM OF FANTASY

THE ENCHANTED CHARMS:
THE SEVENTH ADVENTURE IN THE KINGDOM OF FANTASY

THE PHOENIX OF DESTINY:
AN EPIC KINGDOM OF FANTASY ADVENTURE

THE HOUR OF MAGIC:
THE EIGHTH ADVENTURE IN THE KINGDOM OF FANTASY

THE WIZARD'S WAND:
THE NINTH ADVENTURE IN THE KINGDOM OF FANTASY

THE SHIP OF SECRETS:
THE TENTH ADVENTURE IN THE KINGDOM OF FANTASY

THE DRAGON OF FORTUNE:
AN EPIC KINGDOM OF FANTASY ADVENTURE

THE JOURNEY THROUGH TIME

BACK IN TIME:
THE SECOND JOURNEY THROUGH TIME

THE RACE AGAINST TIME:
THE THIRD JOURNEY THROUGH TIME

LOST IN TIME:
THE FOURTH JOURNEY THROUGH TIME

NO TIME TO LOSE:
THE FIFTH JOURNEY THROUGH TIME